UNVEILING EVIDENCE

Apostle Prof Johnson Suleman

UNVEILING EVIDENCE

Apostle Prof. Johnson Suleman
Copyright@2024

ISBN:

Published in Nigeria by
Hosanna Publishers
Km 132 Benin-Okene/ Abuja Express way,
Auchi, Edo State, Nigeria
Tel: +2348106468478

CONTENTS

INTRODUCTION

We are in the era of evidence. Scripture puts it as a performance of those things God has spoken. It is one thing for the Lord to speak, it is another for the spoken word to become flesh, that which we can see and handle. The enabler of the spoken or written word of God is the Holy Spirit. He is on the scene, available to bring to manifestation the word of God.

Manifestation, however, cannot be birthed or activated except in the place of fervent prayers. When the Holy Spirit an issue, He leads His sons how to pray with groanings that cannot be uttered.

Likewise the Spirit also helpeth our infirmities: for we know not what we should pray for as we ought: but the Spirit itself maketh intercession for us with groanings which cannot be uttered. (Rom.8:26 KJV)

This is a realm of mysteries, where things are turned around, and expectations become a reality.

Stepping into this realm requires an unbroken resolve and readiness to have an intimate relationship with the Holy Spirit. When this is in place, your actions and response to confrontations would not be by guesswork because you would be empowered for every assignment.

And the LORD shall make thee the head, and not the tail; and thou shalt be above only, and thou shalt not be beneath; if that thou hearken unto the commandments of the LORD thy God, which I command thee this day, to observe and to do them: **(Deut 28:13 KJV)**

The above scripture gives up another vital key needed to carry our evidence- obedience. As you read this book, make to decision to walk with the Holy Spirit by taking heed to His word and acting on them. His word will become flesh in your life in Jesus name.

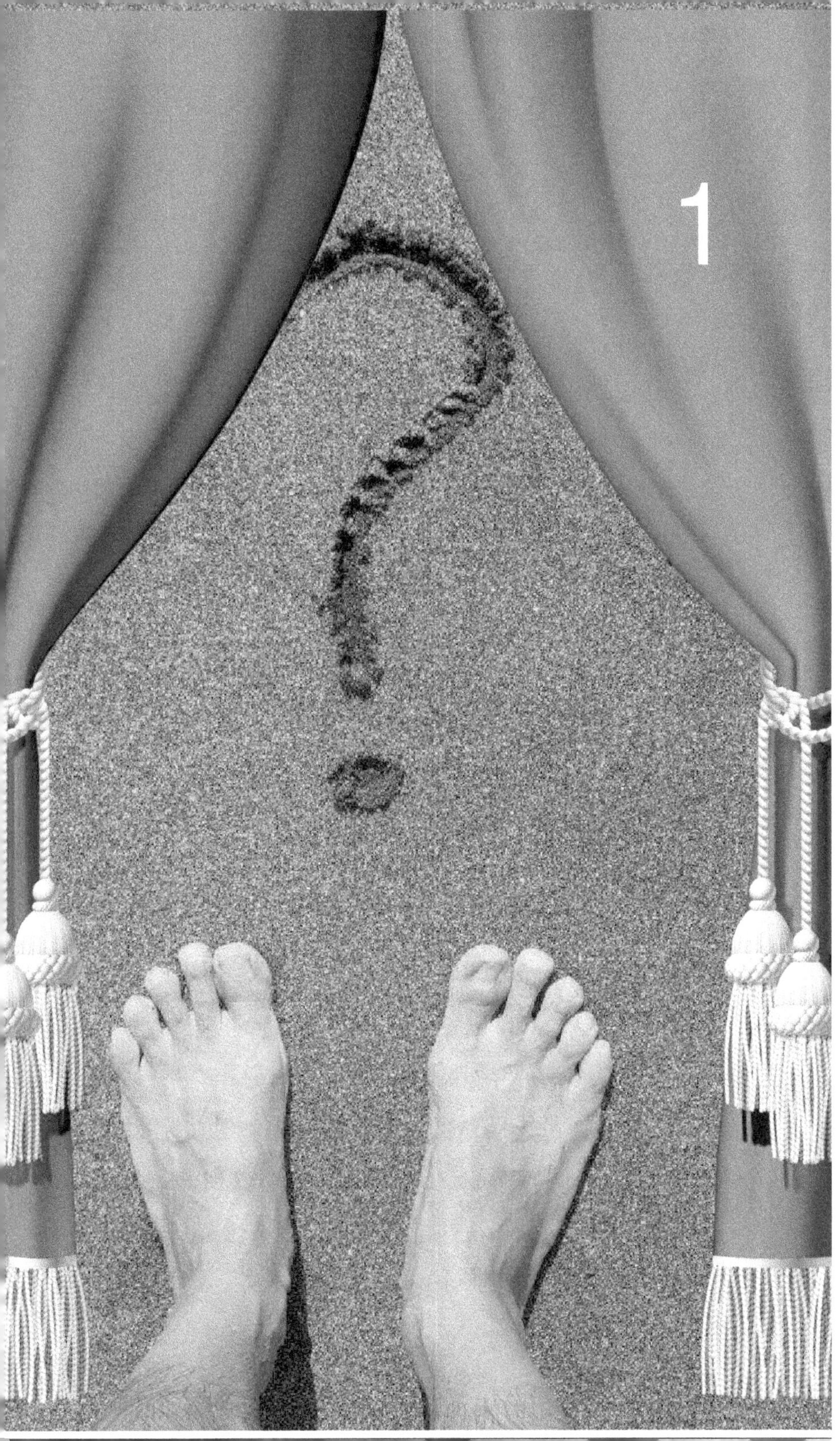

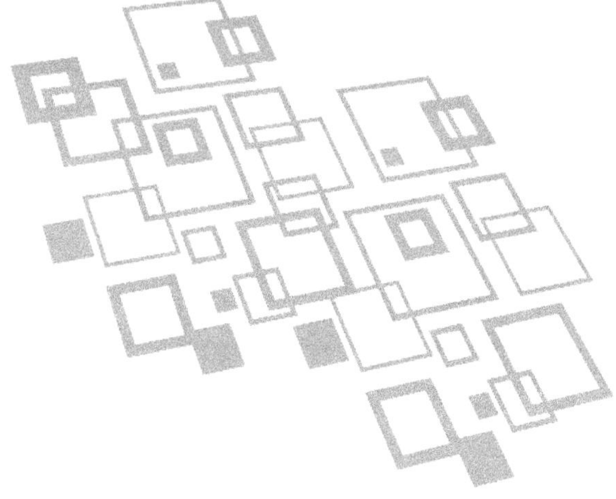

IS THERE A CASE?

*B**ut this is that which was spoken by the prophet Joel;* (**Acts 2.16 KJV**)

The postulation in Acts 2.16 obviously drew attention to another action, event or substance. For anyone to say, "…this is that which was spoken about …", it connotes a reference. What was Peter referring to? Before that question can be answered, let us establish the synonym of the phrase: "This is that…" Any statement or document presented before a group of people or persons to convince, win, or drive home a point is evidence. In legal briefs, the most germane part is the evidence supporting whatever argument is being put forward. If the evidence is defective the case will be muddled up. The man or woman who possesses the evidence is the witness. So, in the anchor verse, it will be correct to say that Apostle Peter was the witness with evidence. We are in the season of manifestations and performances. Not so many believers realize that the statement connotes legal deposition. How do you become a 'performance' when you hold no evidence? You can only manifest if and only when you are the witness.

For the earnest expectation of the creature waiteth for the manifestation of the sons of God. (**Romans 8:19 KJV**)

When the scripture says, "the creature waits for the manifestation of the son of God." It can as well be paraphrased to mean: the sons of God are the holders of the evidences. Actually, in Acts 2.16 Peter made a bold announcement to the world that evidence had been handed over to them. Recall that prior to this episode, Christ Jesus had ascended after crucifixion and resurrection. So, if the apostles must be proof producers, they must be witnesses. Now, who is a witness? Erroneously some people conclude that a witness must be physically present at an event or the scene of the case he/she presents. Though, not entirely wrong, but more importantly, a witness is someone who possesses a piece of evidence. The evidence at your disposal is what qualifies you to be a witness. What evidence was Apostle Peter holding? The usual encounter in Acts 2:1-13 explains this. Prior to Acts 2, a certain prophet Joel had prophesied of the world. Several years after the prophecy, generations patiently waited for it. They expected its fulfillment because they understood the implication.

Nevertheless we, according to his promise, look for new heavens and a new earth, wherein dwelleth righteousness. **(2 Peter 3:13 KJV)**

The Holy Spirit manifests whatever is spoken by God the Father. Countless revelations of the word existed; the people of God anxiously needed manifestations of them. The outpouring in Acts 2 was an announcement of the evidence being handed over. So, is there a case? Yes, there have always been cases before and after the outpouring of the Holy Spirit. To have a case is never an issue. However, it is an issue to have unresolved cases. The disciples could not have resolved or put a stop to the many cases without the presence of the Holy Spirit. The best thing that has happened to the earth is the outpouring of the Holy Ghost. This is the season everything God has spoken is coming to pass.

And blessed is she that believed: for there shall be a performance of those things which were told her from the Lord. (**Luke 1:45 KJV**)

The next logical question all non-dogmatic Christians should ask is how I do partake from the episode of Acts 2? The expression of Luke 1:45 explicitly puts that to rest. You only need to believe. The upper room was beyond an elevated room. It was a realm. Nothing can be fulfilled in the life of any man except the Holy Ghost is released. So, 1st John

1:1-4, completely explains this. To unveil evidence is to handle with your hands those things that God spoke about. When, for instance, the promised baby comes to your hands, you can say this is the evidence. The attack on the witness by the wicked world prompted the Father to send the Holy Ghost. When He sent the prophets, they were killed. The Son was equally killed. So, the evidence was then handed over through the Holy Ghost. The Holy Spirit cannot be killed. How do you kill what you can't see?

"I will not leave you comfortless: I will come to you. Yet a little while, and the world seeth me no more; but ye see me: because I live, ye shall live also." **(John 14:18-19 KJV)**

He is the Word in the Spirit form. The introduction of the Holy Spirit to the scene was because of the extermination of evidence borne by the prophets. Criminals destroy evidence to evade justice. The world benefits from justice and judgments to face out disorderliness. The Father, therefore, protected the evidence in order to salvage the world. No one can manifest except the evidence exists to dispossess the evil one of its place. The devil knows he is an imposition on earth. He pre-tenaciously occupied the place not originally reserved for him. He can't be displaced until the new occupant holds the token into the possession. Man is the god of the earth.

"The heaven, even the heavens, are the LORD's: but the earth hath he given to the children of men." (**Psalms 115:16 KJV**)

"What is man, that thou art mindful of him? and the son of man, that thou visitest him? For thou hast made him a little lower than the angels, and hast crowned him with glory and honour. Thou madest him to have dominion over the works of thy hands; thou hast put all things under his feet" (**Psalms 8:4-6 KJV**)

Nothing comes into the physical world until they are called forth from the spiritual world. Mere mortals can't initiate this transformation. It is the one born of the Spirit that is the son of God. It is only a son of

God who manifests. Aliens to the commonwealth of heaven don't manifest. The outpouring of the Holy Spirit essentially empowers the believer to dispossess the devil of the goods. You can't enter his abode except you first bound him (Mark 3:37). Have you ever wondered why no demon was ever cast out before the arrival of Christ/Holy Spirit? The worst confusion the devil can't decipher is the transformation of man.

In Ephesians 2:6, the believer's position and realm changed. He now operates from the heavenlies. The indwelling of the Holy Spirit goes far beyond the elementary benefit of speaking in tongues. The Holy Spirit indwells in you to take dominion of any field of human endeavour.

Dominion and fear are with him, he maketh peace in his high places. Is there any number of his armies? and upon whom doth not his light arise?* (Job 25:2-3 KJV)

Have you been planted? Where are you planted? You must dominate the mountain where your feet has been founded. Don't localize the operations and boundaries of the Holy Spirit. Beginning from miracles, healings, to the world of engineering and medical sciences, He holds the keys. He is not limited to Sunday's operations and manifestations alone. He created the world. What He can't change does not exist.

Ah Lord GOD! behold, thou hast made the heaven and the earth by thy great power and stretched out arm, and there is nothing too hard for thee: **(Jeremiah 32:17 KJV)**

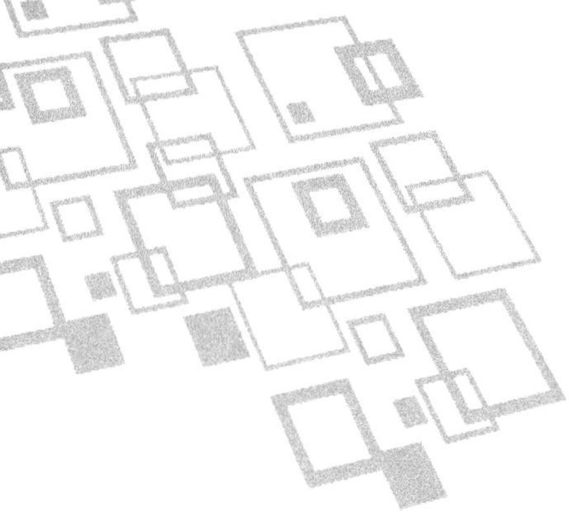

2

...AND THE APOSTLES ACTED

Now Peter and John went up together into the temple at the hour of prayer, being the ninth hour. And a certain man lame from his mother's womb was carried, whom they laid daily at the gate of the temple which is called Beautiful, to ask alms of them that entered into the temple; Who seeing Peter and John about to go into the temple asked an alms. And Peter, fastening his eyes upon him with John, said, Look on us. And he gave heed unto them, expecting to receive something of them. Then Peter said, Silver and gold have I none;

but such as I have give I thee: In the name of Jesus Christ of Nazareth rise up and walk. {Acts 3.1-6 KJV}

The events that followed the Holy Ghost baptism in Acts 2 transformed the globe forever. The upper room was not an elevated building. It was a realm of the Holy Ghost where men of prayer resided. It was not a physical structure. You can't live in prayers, and not act prayers. In Chapter 3, the lame man looked on them (Peter and John) and received an external miracle. Evidence is incontrovertible. The testimony of the man at the beautiful gate could not be disputed. You can't manifest without the Holy Ghost-led prayers. You may afford to pray religiously without the Holy Ghost. If you must change the dynamics of things, He must lead the prayers.

Likewise, the Spirit also helpeth our infirmities: for we know not what we should pray for as we ought: but the Spirit itself maketh intercession for us with groanings which cannot be uttered. {Romans 8.26 KJV}

In Acts 4.31, the place was shaken. Not even at Gethsemane where Christ Jesus desperately needed their support in prayers could they do this. When the Holy Spirit comes prayer points are abundant and time is immaterial. This time, hours were not counted. Beyond speaking in tongues, the change in prayer life is another evidence of the outpouring of the Holy Spirit. How can you be filled with the Holy Spirit and be cold? The church was birthed with tongues of fire, not in a refrigerator. The prayers which re-ordered the earth had begun. The earth will never be the same again. The devil can only own man if man lies. So, in chapter 5, he infiltrated Ananias first. Soon after the wife, Sapphira was not spared. They were roasted in fire with no physical trace outside the dead bodies. The same anointing that blesses equally consumes. When the power of God manifests the footprints are noticeable for no one to doubt. And fear came on the church.

And great fear came upon all the church, and upon as many as heard these things. And by the hands of the apostles were many signs and wonders wrought among the people; (and they were all with one accord in Solomon's porch. {**Acts 5:11-12 KJV**}

When evidence is delivered, miracles are in abundance. The anointing does not just judge, it multiplies in exponential propensity (Acts 5. 14). The same timid disciples who feared for their lives had taken over the space. When the Holy Ghost comes, fear disappears. Miracles take the stage.

Do you know what? Unprecedented abundance set in, men and women of wisdom are known in times of scarcity or abundance. The appointment of Stephen and the other six gave them focus. They could not afford to abandon the fire and serve tables. It is always better to act and make mistakes than to remain docile. Was Stephen really supposed to be ordained a deacon or an evangelist? Being filled with Holy Ghost, Stephen preached to the Jewish leaders, though stoned. In verse 59, Stephen said, "… Lord Jesus receive my spirit".

And said, Behold, I see the heavens opened, and the Son of man standing on the right hand of God. Then they cried out with a loud voice, and stopped their ears, and ran upon him with one accord, And cast him out of the city, and stoned him: and the witnesses laid down their clothes at a young man's feet, whose name was Saul. And they stoned Stephen, calling upon God, and saying, Lord Jesus, receive my spirit. And he kneeled down, and cried with a loud voice, Lord, lay not this sin to their charge. And when he had said this, he fell asleep. {**Acts 7:56-60 KJV**}

Did Stephen really understand what it meant for the Son of Man to be seen standing on the right hand of God? Christ Jesus sits normally. When He stood, He did to defend Stephen. He can't work for you except you let Him. Saul spearheaded the painful exit of Stephen. Saul later became Paul and paid the price all through his ministry. Don't permit anyone to take your life, they might repent later. Nevertheless, every action attracts appropriate consequences. This entire prognosis is to show how tangible the evidence became. No one could argue the transformation at the upper room.

Let us briefly consider areas to pay some attention to when the anointing comes.

(1) Your words

***Death and life are in the power of the tongue: and they that love it shall eat the fruit thereof.* {Proverbs 18:21 KJV}**

Though, this is true for all. But, specially so for the anointed. Stephen's death could have been averted. He prayed a wrong prayer. Whatever you call for is what the angels execute. In Ecclesiastes 5.6, the Holy Spirit forewarned us to be careful what we utter out of our mouths. Once you are anointed, the angels take instructions from you via the words of your mouth. What you say is what you become. Don't speak death. Proclaim life; declare excellence and perfection, it will be the order of the day around you. Your words activate your angels. They are permanently deployed to watch and attend to you.

The more conscious you are of their presence the better your safety and wellbeing are guaranteed. Your responsibility is to make declarations, theirs is to execute. So, do your part.

(2) The Anointed is Untouchable

***Saying, Touch not mine anointed, and do my prophets no harm**. {**Psalm 105:15 KJV**}*

Be extremely circumspect in how you conduct yourself around the anointed. The God of the anointed is also a consuming fire. It is a command not to "touch" or "do the prophet any arm." Obey it. One wonders what devastation happened to the killers of Stephen, if the mastermind paid so many prices. Christ Jesus encountered Saul (Paul) who supervised the death of Stephen. Perhaps, he was anointed to complete the assignment of Stephen with persecution added to the cup. Paul faced unspeakable humiliations almost throughout his earthly ministry.

In I Samuel 26.9, David spared the life of Saul, because he understood the anger of God concerning its violation. He restrained Abishai from touching Saul. For every obedience to the act of God, there is a blessing.

In Psalm 2.2, in fact, God equates touching His anointed to attempting Him. It is as severe as that. Who battles with the Lord says the songwriter? Certainly, no one succeeds at that. There are things never to be contemplated. Though, it might take time sometimes, certainly the repercussions always come.

The kings of the earth set themselves, and the rulers take counsel together, against the LORD, and against his anointed, saying, {Psalm 2:2 KJV}

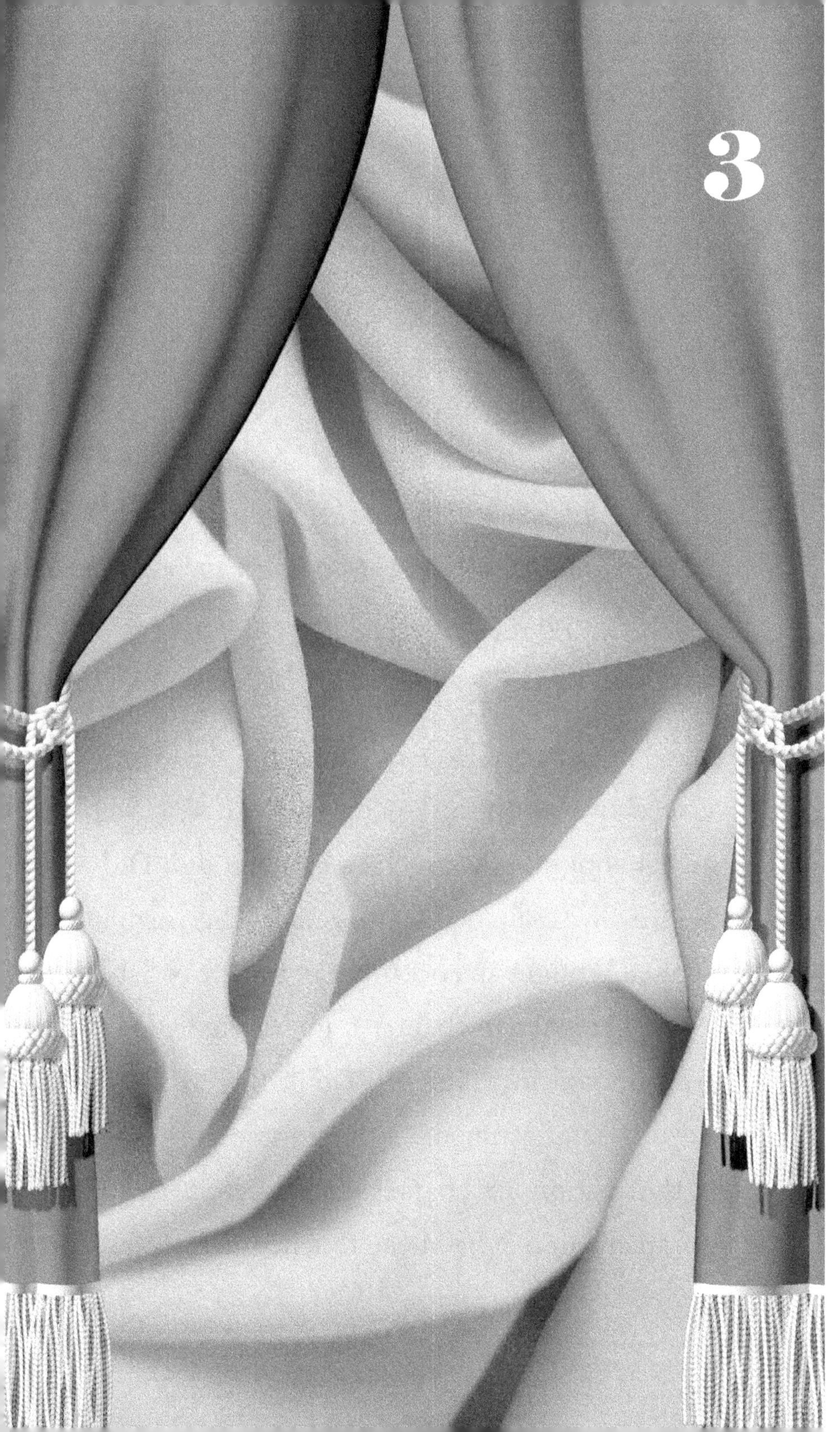
3

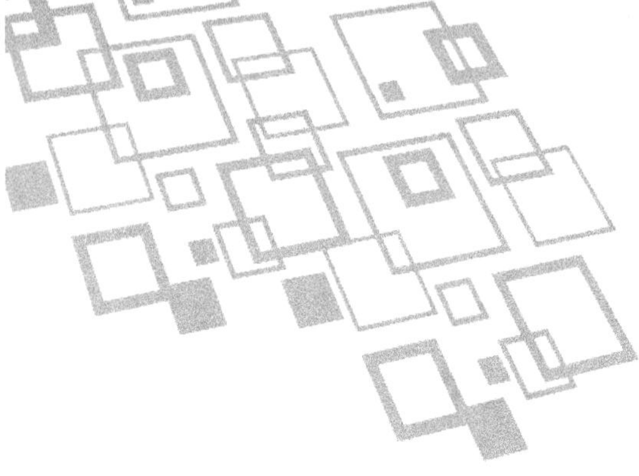

And cast him out of the city, and stoned him: and the witnesses laid down their clothes at a young man's feet, whose name was Saul. {**Acts 7:58 KJV**}

There are scriptural verses you don't gloss over. The verse above is one of such. The cloth of Stephen carried anointing as much as Stephen did. Did Saul go away without being impacted? The garment of Stephen brought an encounter in the life of Saul. The death of Stephen in chapter 7, undoubtedly led to the arrest of Saul in chapter 9. Don't forget that Philip had demonstrated uncommon spiritual transformation in chapter 8. In Acts 8.26-40, the Ethiopian eunuch had been touched to transfer same to the continent of Africa. The spread of wildfire was unstoppable. Divinity ordered the steps of the disciples to spread the gospel within a short time. After the queen of Sheba had contact with Solomon and returned home with great impartation, here comes another. This time around, the fire of the Holy Ghost with evidence to witness the gospel had stormed the continent of Africa. What initially appeared like cloven tongues on 120 disciples had begun to grow in multi–dimensional proportions.

And believers were the more added to the Lord, multitudes both of men and women.) Insomuch that they brought forth the sick into the streets, and laid them on beds and couches, that at the least the shadow of Peter passing by might overshadow some of them. There came also a multitude out of the cities round about unto Jerusalem, bringing sick folks, and them which were vexed with unclean spirits: and they were healed everyone. {Acts 5:14-16 KJV}

"What shall you have me do?" of Acts 9.6a commenced the unquantifiable proportion of the move of God. Your level of devotion determines the expression of the Holy Ghost through the individual. Again, Cornelius had a great encounter due to much devotion. What was Cornelius devoted to? He made his family to follow God. If the service of man could draw the attention of God, then, he displayed uncommon and selfless service. Sometimes, beyond the service, the motive matters more. Many people have been frustrated from doing good works because of the responses. If you look forward to the applause of man, you can hardly please God. Every good gesture must first be directed to God before the direct recipient. Cornelius was given to prayers. He was referred to Peter to receive the simplification of the prayer. He routinely kept to prayers despite not having received the Holy Ghost.

Another interesting dimension to study about the life of Cornelius is the effective combination of spirituality with wealth. Much possession of money is never an excuse for carnality. Cornelius was a man of great influence and still had time for God.

There was a certain man in Caesarea called Cornelius, a centurion of the band called the Italian band, A devout man, and one that feared God with all his house, which gave much alms to the people, and prayed to God always. {Acts 10:1-2 KJV}

Have you once shown interest in the things of God? Has it dwindled because of your rise in politics or business? Being a career, academics, or security expert should not diminish your value for the things of God. The primary concern of God is to partner with us. He must want you to take over the security, medical, academics, and political sphere. He wants to use your Ass to reign in the city triumphantly. When you partner with Him, He shines through you. The donkey Christ Jesus rode on in Matthew 21.1-19, walked on the cloths. Those who wanted to touch Christ Jesus equally had to inevitably touch the donkey. This is the symbiotic relationship that exists between God and every vessel of His. The anointing brings exposure, speed, and unequaled direction. You can't be anointed and be confused.

And Abram was very rich in cattle, in silver, and in gold. {**Genesis 13:2 KJV**}

You can be a prayer addict and be stupendously rich. Gone are the days of wrong misconceptions that service to God was synonymous to lack. It is a deception of hell. You can be spiritual and be wealthy. The tradition of men would have made it impossible for Cornelius to set up. Without the Holy Ghost, a permanent limit is placed on you.

In Acts 10:44-45, God went ahead of the expectation of man. The Holy Ghost is not for a sect in Christianity. He is for everyone who must exhibit uncommon exploits. The Jews in the days of Peter had parochial understanding of the essence and workings of the Holy Ghost. They summoned Peter in verses 2-3 of Acts Chapter 11, demanding explanations of his encounter with Cornelius. If God followed the human trajectory, the Holy Ghost would have been hoarded. The Holy Ghost is the carrier of the evidence. The gospel must spread amongst all tribes and tongues.

And he said unto them, Go ye into all the world, and preach the gospel to every creature. {**Mark 16:15 KJV**}

The Holy Ghost came for every creed and language. If you believe in the Lordship of Christ, you can receive Him. He needs you to witness in the offices and parks over the globe. Sometimes, the battles we fight are generated by people around us. The Jewish believers were against Peter because of Cornelius. Paul and Barnabas were torn apart because of John Mark and Silas. Anyway, let us consider how a believer can stay away from a life of controversy to devotion. Whatever you give attention to grows.

(1) Humble yourself and pray

Humility is not timidity. It is equally not being sanctimonious. Nothing demonstrates the life of humility like prayers. Prayer is an admission of the limitation of man and the supremacy of God. Except you master the invitation of God into your affairs, things remain the same. Change is not wished or desired, it is acted on until you take a step of faith to begin what you may never finish. Have you begun to pray? Prayer is an unending relationship with God. The humility Cornelius showed through prayers attracted God. God still refers His prophets to men; the difference is the prayer life.

"If my people, which are called by my name, shall humble themselves, and pray, and seek my face, and turn from their wicked ways; then will I hear from heaven, and will forgive their sin, and will heal their land." (2 Chronicles 7:14 KJV)

God seems far when prayer is scarce. The drought of prayers is the presence of hopelessness. Discrimination is an issue when men recommend you. When God gives your address to the Peters, no one can restrain them. When issues are settled in the secrets, favour is enjoyed in the open. It takes nothing to pray, just know without Him you can do little. Barriers are broken when God becomes your referral. It would have taken Cornelius endless lobby to ever gain access to Peter. Only prayers destroy the tradition of men. If you can pray, you can live above men-imposed limits. One of the primary assignments of the Holy Ghost is intercessory. If you can't pray, He can't abide with you.

Likewise the Spirit also helpeth our infirmities: for we know not what we should pray for as we ought: but the Spirit itself maketh intercession for us with groanings which cannot be uttered. And he that searcheth the hearts knoweth what is the mind of the Spirit, because he maketh intercession for the saints according to the will of God. {Romans 8:26-27 KJV}

(2) Do for others

In Matthew 7.12, Christ Jesus said, "Therefore, whatever you want men to do to you, do also to them". The early Apostles saw the extraordinary move of God because they lived the word. Cornelius stepped out of his comfort zone to make life better for others. Little do you wonder why God disrupted Peter's programs to make his better? There is nothing we do in the name of God that will not receive the commensurate reward. Men may take advantage, but

God takes notice. We are often frustrated because we focus on the wrong reasons. Let Him know you are acting in obedience to His word.

"And whosoever shall give to drink unto one of these little ones a cup of cold water only in the name of a disciple, verily I say unto you, he shall in no wise lose his reward." {**Matthew 10:42 KJV**}

4

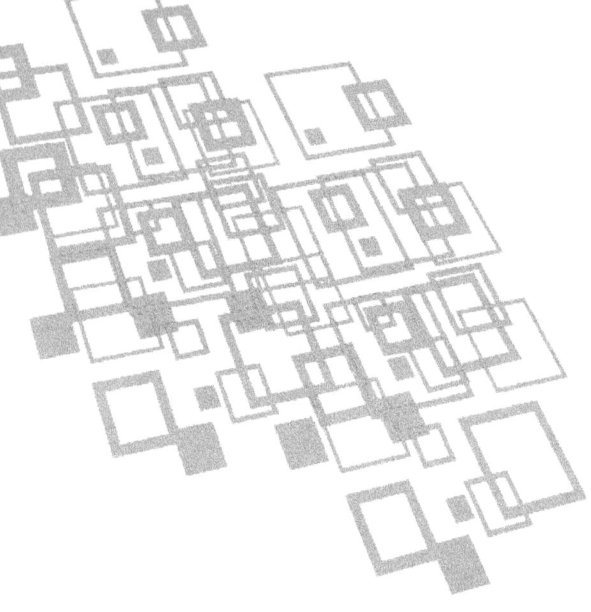

EVIDENCE OR IMITATION?

And there were seven sons of one Sceva, a Jew, and chief of the priests, which did so. And the evil spirit answered and said, Jesus I know, and Paul I know; but who are ye? And the man in whom the evil spirit was leaped on them, and overcame them, and prevailed against them, so that they fled out of that house naked and wounded. And this was known to all the Jews and Greeks also dwelling at Ephesus; and fear fell on them all, and the name of the Lord Jesus was magnified. {Acts **19:14-17 KJV**}

If the genuine exist, the counterfeit must be in circulation side-by-side. The consequence of being in possession of some fake products is what deters people. If there are no punishments for possessing fake, it spreads. The seven sons of Sceva did not first estimate the consequences of faking the evidence. They were not witnesses, nor did they have access to the Holy Ghost. Casting the demon out goes beyond the shout. The seven sons of one Sceva mistook their religious practices for possession of evidence. One of the reasons people misbehave is the assumption, rightly or wrongly, of no immediate retribution. Obviously, these children had mastered the act of religious practices from their father. Unfortunately, this time around they got it wrong. Imitation may carry you some places, certainly not the strong man's abode. You need to be empowered to enter the territory of the strong man. Spiritual things are never trial and error.

"No man can enter into a strong man's house, and spoil his goods, except he will first bind the strong

man; and then he will spoil his house." {**Mark 3:27 KJV**}

The demonic spirit knew Jesus and Paul. The identity of the sons of Sceva was unknown. When the Holy Ghost is not present, evidence is absent. The demons were simply asking the sons of Sceva to produce the token of being sent. Imagine walking up to an immigration post without the necessary documents. How do you fly into a country you have not obtained a visa to enter? It's a total violation of spiritual protocols for the sons of Sceva to have attempted to command the demons. In the realm of the spirit, there are different ranks. Ranks are not self-imposed. They are conferred on the possessors by the authorizing body. It would not have attracted any monetary cost for them to acquire the Holy Ghost. Perhaps, if records like this don't exist, several people may have seen spiritual things as a game of chance. Spiritual warfare is not by power or might. One demonic person messed up seven able-bodied men cheaply.

Now Moses kept the flock of Jethro his father in law, the priest of Midian: and he led the flock to the backside of the desert, and came to the mountain of God, even to Horeb. And the angel of the LORD appeared unto him in a flame of fire out of the midst of a bush: and he looked, and, behold, the bush burned with fire, and the bush was not consumed. And Moses said, I will now turn aside, and see this great sight, why the bush is not burnt. {Exodus 3:1-3 KJV}

Moses understood the importance of evidence. When the bush burned, his attention was sought. Moses didn't jump at the errand of God. He carefully needed indisputable evidence. You can only gamble like the sons of Sceva, if you have not been embarrassed before. Never underrate an enemy. Moses had previously made an attempt at parading non-existing evidence. You will recall, according to Exodus 2.11-20, Moses killed an Egyptian. The difference between his first attempt and the successful emancipation of the Israelites is evidence.

He lacked the evidence because he was not empowered. Only the sent ones are empowered. Have you been sent? You know the people you are sent to. The outpouring of the Holy Ghost is not for intimidating people. You are endowed to liberate others.

Now the sojourning of the children of Israel, who dwelt in Egypt, was four hundred and thirty years. And it came to pass at the end of the four hundred and thirty years, even the selfsame day it came to pass, that all the hosts of the LORD went out from the land of Egypt. It is a night to be much observed unto the LORD for bringing them out from the land of Egypt: this is that night of the LORD to be observed of all the children of Israel in their generations. **{Exodus 12:40-42 KJV}**

Every genuine endowment is for liberation. When the fire comes on you, you will be energized for the work. The supernatural ability of divinity is fully deployed. The apostles achieved so much, within a limited space. Moses broke the yoke that lasted for

430 years within a little while. Men struggle because the Holy Ghost is not present. He is the enabler of speed in life and destiny. How much you know Him is how far you go. Are you ready? When Cornelius was ready his actions showed it. Verbal readiness is not as important as actionable readiness.

For if any be a hearer of the word, and not a doer, he is like unto a man beholding his natural face in a glass: For he beholdeth himself, and goeth his way, and straightway forgetteth what manner of man he was. But whoso looketh into the perfect law of liberty, and continueth therein, he being not a forgetful hearer, but a doer of the work, this man shall be blessed in his deed. {James 1:23-25 KJV}

Those that are sent make things appear easy and attractive. Imitate no man. Standing on your lane and remaining focused triggers the partnership with the Holy Ghost. Moses approached Egypt with an uncommon audacity. When the "I am that I am" sends you, the Pharaohs are immaterial. The confidence of Moses stemmed from the encounter at the burning bush. Have you had an encounter? All that you need to turn things around is an encounter. Daniel resolved within himself to be an outstanding personality. If you have not left anything, you can't command forces.

But Daniel purposed in his heart that he would not defile himself with the portion of the king's. meat, nor with the wine which he drank: therefore he requested of the prince of the eunuchs that he might not defile himself. {Daniel 1:8 KJV}

Intimacy with God stimulates favour from men. No man will do anything meaningful until God compels them. God compelled Peter to attend to Cornelius. Barnabas took the matter of Paul upon himself because God remotely engineered it (Acts 9.27). Barnabas enabled the acceptance of Paul the Apostle before the early church. Paul the Apostle needed their acceptance to further the propagation of the gospel. Men are readily at your disposal when the touch of the Lord comes. The fire of God prepares the way for the actualization of the assignment. The fire delivers both the human and the material resources.

Daniel was intelligent and resourceful. His usefulness was utilized by several kings (Daniel 1.21 and Daniel 5.11-12). Being outstanding is never by chance. Who you meet determines the message you deliver. The content of his advice remained relevant. You can't fade off the scene if you possess the original. One of the evidence of original products is durability. Whoever discountenances original products does so at their own peril. Can what work be substituted? You can't be connected to the source and not deliver the right product. There is a specification the world requires from you. In Egypt, the Israelites received nothing but deliverance from bondage. Nothing else would have made any realistic meaning than the liberation they needed. Attention comes on you when you possess the needs of the people. Your usefulness is limited without meeting with the Lord first. Every good and lasting gift begins from the bosom of God.

Every good gift and every perfect gift is from above, and cometh down from the Father of lights, with whom is no variableness, neither shadow of turning. {James 1:17 KJV}

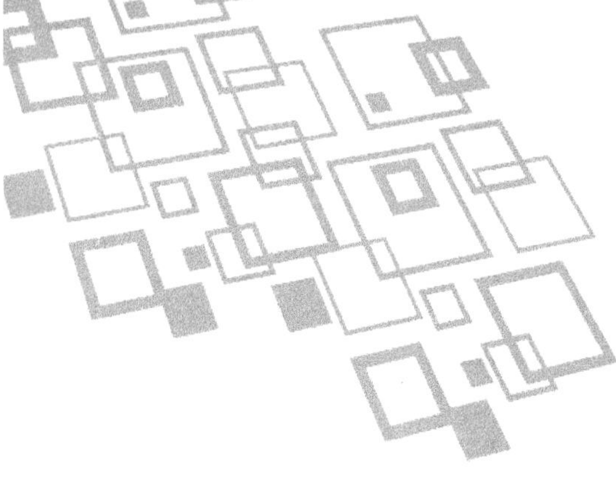

5

THE TRANSFORMATION

And the spirit of the LORD shall rest upon him, the spirit of wisdom and understanding, the spirit of counsel and might, the spirit of knowledge and of the fear of the LORD; {Isaiah 11.2 KJV}

But if the Spirit of him that raised up Jesus from the dead dwell in you, he that raised up Christ from the dead shall also quicken your mortal bodies by his Spirit that dwelleth in you. {Romans 8.11 KJV}

The Holy Ghost enables transformation. However, I have often opined, any aspiration which leaves the greater responsibility in the hands of God is irresponsibility. The Holy Ghost will not engineer your transformation except you prepare a room for it. A lot of believers erroneously presume that the Holy Ghost comes to abdicate their duties. According to Charles. R. Swindoll; "Life is 10% what happens to you and 90% how you react to it." Have you ever paused to consider what happened to several other disciples who were present in the upper room? The baptism of the Holy Spirit is not one of the religious rituals. As excellent as speaking in tongues is, it is only the foundation. Who will celebrate a foundation of about 10 years old without any noticeable progress? That you speak in tongues fluently after spending more than 5 years in a local Assembly is not progressive. He is not a feel-good hormone. He came to enable you accomplish a task.

For what man knoweth the things of a man, save the spirit of man which is in him? even so the things of God knoweth no man, but the Spirit of God. {I Cor. 2:11 KJV}

The worst scenario is those who have no concrete plans or aspirations. John 14:26 says, "…the Holy

Ghost will remind you of all things…" He can't remind you if He didn't teach you. Do teachers revise the subjects or topics they never taught? To remind is to revise. And of course, you can't be taught except you set out to learn. That act of learning is an intentional one. Teachers don't force students to learn. Students approach schools and enroll to be taught. What task of transformation is before you that the Holy Ghost can teach you? Have you enrolled in the school of the Holy Ghost? The presumption that things will work in the right direction because of the outpoured unction on you is wrong. Nothing will change until you set out to change them. Your life is your task. The Holy Spirit is your senior partner. What you prepare for is what He will assist you on.

For it is God which worketh in you both to will and to do of his good pleasure. {**Philippians 2:13 KJV**}

Apart from disciples like Stephen, Philip, and Peter, the numerous others were never seen in the available records. Do you also want to fade away unread? Even if one lives on earth for 1000 years, it is few compared to the enormity of the assignment ahead. The easiest way to destroy tomorrow is to postpone today. Tomorrow can't shine except today is prepared for. The Lord instructed the disciples to go to the upper room for prayers. Could He not have impacted them there? Must they go to the upper room? Every genuine move of God will be predicated on previous sacrifice. No seed sprouts if it does not fall to the ground first. Seeds would have preferred silos where they can live longer untouched. Your silo is your comfort zone. Transformation requires great discomfort. It is never easy to pursue greatness. Certainly, the disciples of Christ Jesus were more than 120. Unfortunately, only 120 disciples proceeded to the upper room.

"Nevertheless, I tell you the truth; It is expedient for you that I go away: for if I go not away, the Comforter will not come unto you; but if I depart, I will send him unto you. And when he is come, he will reprove the world of sin, and of righteousness, and of judgment:" {John 16:7-8 KJV}

It might not be surprising to find some argue and rationalize that without the upper room the outpouring can still come. Or, where else did the others go? Peradventure some undermined the principle of rising. If a resounding breakthrough must be recorded, you must first separate yourself. They needed to stay away from the distractions of the world. Remember, this happened in the festive season. It takes extreme determination to stay off ceremony and focus on prayers. It is unlikely that some disciples joined the ceremony of Pentecost rather than abide together in one accord in the upper room. Which would you have joined?

This I say then, walk in the Spirit, and ye shall not fulfil the lust of the flesh. {**Galatians 5:16 KJV**}

The fire at the burning bush came for Moses' transformation. You can't lead except you are transformed. It is a mandatory pathway everyone on a mission must pass. Noah spearheaded the leadership of the earth. The encounter he had made it possible. You can't drive a value system you have not been empowered to lead. Justice, fairness, and righteousness didn't get obliterated from the earth, because Noah was secured. Imitation never goes far. There is a fundamental fabric that the Holy Ghost implants in us. You can stand because the fire has stood on you. When Peter and John told the lame at the beautiful gate, "look on us," they knew they had been impacted. The audacity came from their previous encounter. They did not need an appraisal of how serious or unserious the situation was. They understood the Holy Ghost was present with them. He was there to execute their command.

Thus saith the LORD, the Holy One of Israel, and his Maker, Ask me of things to come concerning my sons, and concerning the work of my hands command ye me. I have made the earth, and created man upon it: I, even my hands, have stretched out the heavens, and all their host have I commanded. {Isaiah 45:11-12 KJV}

You represent the King of kings if you have been endowed by the Holy Ghost. Be separated into the upper room, so you can shine. Separation precedes the fire and thereafter the shining. The misstep is that countless people run after the shining. Great people pursue vision and greatness comes after them. The easiest indicator of fakeness is the pursuit of greatness. Elijah never wanted to be great, but to enjoy Him and correct societal ills. Situations fall in place when you're within the mandate. The evidence you possess determines the court session you appear in. You can never be assigned to all cases. The judge will discountenance you when your evidence is not relevant to the case at hand. Who have you been sent to rescue? It is worse if the target is unknown. The beginning of speed is the visualization of the destination in mind. Everyone is sent to somebody. The IT giants have been sent to solve the problems of information technology. Smith Wigglesworth was baptized to influence the history of Pentecostalism. The birth of Kathryn Kuhlman revolutionized the healing ministry. No one was genuinely in doubt of the anointing on her life. She was outstanding and spectacular in her friendship and display of communion with the Holy Spirit. In similar vein, men and women have been sent to transform different mountains. Those sent to the aviation industry, for instance, should ensure the presence of the Holy Spirit is never in doubt. Do it, you can.

And he gave some, apostles; and some, prophets; and some, evangelists; and some, pastors and teachers; For the perfecting of the saints, for the work of the ministry, for the edifying of the body of Christ: Till we all come in the unity of the faith, and of the knowledge of the Son of God, unto a perfect man, unto the measure of the stature of the fulness of Christ: That we henceforth be no more children, tossed to and fro, and carried about with every wind of doctrine, by the sleight of men, and cunning craftiness, whereby they lie in wait to deceive; {Ephesians 4:11-14 KJV

6

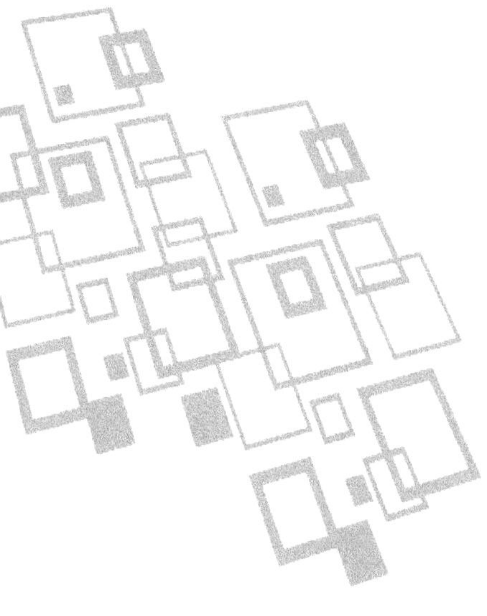

CHANGE YOUR MIND

I beseech you therefore, brethren, by the mercies of God, that ye present your bodies a living sacrifice, holy, acceptable unto God, which is your reasonable service. And be not conformed to this world: but be ye transformed by the renewing of your mind, that ye may prove what is that good, and acceptable, and perfect, will of God. {Romans 12:1-2 KJV}

The outpouring of the Holy Spirit comes to transform the Spirit man. I suppose, it is a settled fact; a man is made of Spirit, mind (soul) and body. Until there is a synergy amongst these three components, little or nothing can be achieved. One of the fulcrums of Christ Jesus messages was repentance according to Mark 1:15. Unfortunately, several people understand repentance to mean conversion. It does not mean conversion from one religion to another at all. The actual Greek translated into repentance is "Kenosis". Kenosis means to empty out of self; to change one's mindset. Now, except the mind is prepared and made ready, it can't house the evidence. The mind does not get born again neither does it receive the Holy Ghost baptism. If you don't empty out your mind with/by the word of God, it cannot comprehend the evidence. It can't operate with it, cannot understand. The mind must be debunked of several debris. It takes the word to train the mind.

Not by works of righteousness which we have done, but according to his mercy he saved us, by the washing of regeneration, and renewing of the Holy Ghost; {Titus 3:5 KJV}

The activities of the Spirit are entirely spiritual. A carnal mind can't understand them. The ordinary man operates in the realm of logic. Logic is an operational level of the mind. However, spiritual things are beyond logical reasoning. Have you not encountered people who sincerely subject spiritual impulse to factual checks? Facts are good, but the truth is higher than facts. Some things are factual but not truthful. The Holy Spirit can't relate with you if your mind is still at the low level of logic. You must upgrade the mind. Did you say how? How did Elisha know his Syrian invaders will be blind in II Kings 6:18-23? Have you ever considered what transpired between Elisha and the servant in II Kings 6:17? Until permission was granted by heaven, they could see nothing. The servant was in the realm of logic. Those who rationalize spiritual dimensions exist here.

(For we walk by faith, not by sight:) {**II Cor. 5:7 KJV**}

Life is beyond what you see. The mind forms an opinion based on the information it is exposed to over time. If a child is never told about the danger of snakes, he/she will grow up never to fear snakes. Similarly, "Kenosis" can only take place by often trafficking in the spirit. The mistake of the seven sons of Sceva is that while they lived in the ordinary, they faked the "Kenosis." It can't be faked. How much of the word do you study and allow to operate in you? The word of God is your wings in the spirit. You can't fly when you are bereft of the word. If the law of aerodynamics negates the law of gravity, why do you mentally resolve how the dead rises?

Thy word is a lamp unto my feet, and a light unto my path. {**Psalm 119.105 KJV**}

These are spiritual realities and truths. They are well settled. What you feed on is what you become. Any information you stay off appears not to exist. The closer you move to God, the nearer He comes to you. Apostle Paul was never doubtful whether Elymas would be blind. Footballers don't doubt whether the object (ball), they kicked up will return back. Repeated occurrence of it has established the faith of it. The evidence Apostle Paul received in Acts 9.1-9 continued to manifest in Acts 13.7-12.

But Elymas the sorcerer (for so is his name by interpretation) withstood them, seeking to turn away the deputy from the faith. Then Saul, (who also is called Paul,) filled with the Holy Ghost, set his eyes on him. And said, O full of all subtilty and all mischief, thou child of the devil, thou enemy of all righteousness, wilt thou not cease to pervert the right ways of the Lord? And now, behold, the hand of the Lord is upon thee, and thou shalt be blind, not seeing the sun for a season. And immediately there fell on him a mist and a darkness; and he went about seeking some to lead him by the hand. {Acts 13.8-11 KJV}

We shall study the strongest enemies of spiritual realities and growth. You can't grow if you can't overcome these enemies.

(1) Doubt

A doubtful mind is a double-minded one. According to the report of Matthew 14.29-33, Peter walked on the sea as long as he held onto the Master's instruction. Soon afterwards, he began to contemplate. The most simplified definition of doubt is contemplation on alternatives. If you still have available options, you can hardly go far in the spiritual things. Why reconsider the voice of God to you in the closet when faced with contrary views of mortal men?

A double minded man is unstable in all his ways. {James 1.8 KJV}

Burn the bridges and move up higher. You can't look up and view down simultaneously. According to John 3.27, your delivery comes from above. So, if your attention is not focused on that same direction, how can you receive? Where you invest is where you harvest. You don't try God. He is the last bus stop. Let your reliance on Him be total. If you approach Him at emergency moments, you can hardly overcome doubt. The God you know in the secret is the one who works for you in the public. Don't let need drive you to Him. Approach Him out of love and friendship. Until your mind is made up like Shadrack, Meshach and Abednego in Daniel 3.16-18, change will be elusive. The love and friendship for the Master didn't allow them contemplate bowing to another god. Whether God saved them or not was never a prerequisite for steadfastness. Stop praying to God because you have an upcoming program. Adopt a lifestyle of prayers and fasting. So, program or not, be consistent.

And he came out, and went, as he was wont, to the mount of Olives; and his disciples also followed him. {Luke 22.39 KJV}

(2) Fear

You must overcome fear to be a man of the spirit. Don't allow fear have hold on you. Fear is mindfulness of being put to shame. In II Kings 6, palpable fear gripped the servant of Elisha. He didn't want disgrace. The fastest antidote to fear is confrontation. Do what you fear. There are about 365 'fear not' in the Bible. If the devil says, suppose the lame does not walk? Reply him, suppose he/she walks? David advanced towards Goliath to counter any possible fear of the uncircumcised Philistine. The

Goliath you defeat today will fear you tomorrow.

Fear thou not; for I am with thee: be not dismayed; for I am thy God: I will strengthen thee; yea, I will help thee; yea, I will uphold thee with the right hand of my righteousness. {Isaiah 41.10 KJV}

Therefore, combat Goliath today without any hesitation. Avoid repeat matches. Go after the task and put the victory behind you. You are not fighting for victory, but from victory. Your life is a replay match. The scores are already on the scoreboard ever before the contest began. You have been declared victorious. The creator of the universe said, "...I am with you, even to the end..." What can be more reassuring than this? He is totally committed to His word.

Then said the LORD unto me, Thou hast well seen: for I will hasten my word to perform it. {Jeremiah 1.12 KJV}

7

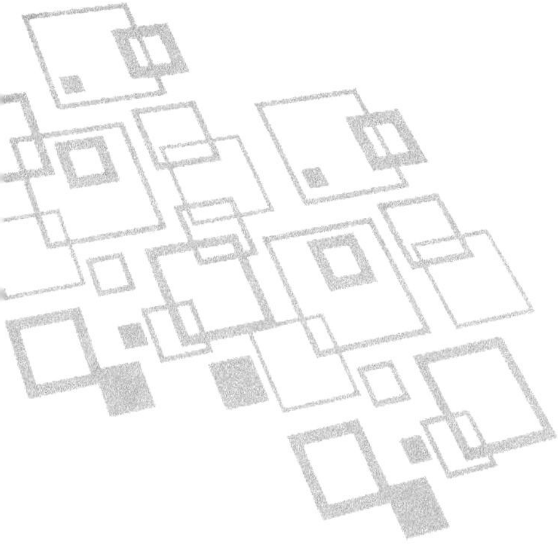

WHERE TO FIND ANSWERS

And call ye on the name of your gods, and I will call on the name of the LORD: and the God that answereth by fire, let him be God. And all the people answered and said, It is well spoken. {I Kings 18.24 KJV}

Call unto me, and I will answer thee, and show thee great and mighty things, which thou knowest not. {Jeremiah 33.3 KJV}

Your answers are hidden in your challenges. Results are found in insults. If you run away from challenges, you can't be the champion. Life is a battlefield. You don't need to be troublesome before one locates your address. There are no vacant thrones. Someone must vacate the throne for a new king to be coronated. In coronation ceremonies, some mourn, and others celebrate. The world won't give you a chance willingly. It is yours to take it. Even Saul, who desperately needed Goliath dead turned around to discourage David. Learn to encourage yourself in the Lord. Always live to prove the nay-sayers wrong. That it has not been done before is the more reason why you should break the jinx. This kingdom does not entertain excuses. Go for the result. Overcoming the obstacles is the least expectation.

For ever, O LORD, thy word is settled in heaven. **{Psalm 119:89 KJV}**

You are designed to break the negative record in that family. You have been sent to validate the evidence. Whatsoever plays out now will be in your favour at the end. Your destiny was already concluded in heaven. If God releases you into the earth, it is because your reliability is guaranteed. There is a warranty on you that cannot fail. In heaven, God tested you and dismembered you to be sent to the earth. You were found dependable and wonderful. You were found prosperous. Before you came as a child you were already an adult. You are not struggling to be successful; you are merely acting out the process. There may be awful ups and downs, but the eventual result is victorious. He told Jeremiah, "… when you were in your mother's womb, I knew thee." How can someone be a prophet in the womb? Obviously, that expression was unveiling the capacity of Jeremiah at installation.

Before I formed thee in the belly, I knew thee; and before thou camest forth out of the womb I sanctified thee, and I ordained thee a prophet unto the nations. **{Jeremiah 1:5 KJV}**

God can't create or release defective products. If you were not working, He won't release you. He sent you because all the capabilities are fully in-built within you. Just the way products like phones are powered, despite being qualitative, you still need to power yourself. Some people fail to work, because they have neglected powering their lives. No matter how sophisticated a new phone is, for instance, if it is not powered by the final consumer it cannot work. Powering your life is a process you must go through. God couldn't have sent you here to be poor. Activate your prosperity He has released already. Most people focus on the fall of Adam than the death and resurrection of Christ. According to Revelation 13:8, the Lamb was slain before the foundation of the earth. What does that mean? The solution predates the problem.

And all that dwell upon the earth shall worship him, whose names are not written in the book of life of the Lamb slain from the foundation of the world. **{Revelation 13:8 KJV}**

We should celebrate our competence which comes before the struggle. Again, one of the inevitable processes of activating your life is via speaking in tongues. Satan understands all human languages except speaking in tongues. He can't stop your prayers. By the way, this world is spiritual. You must download your progress from the spirit world. The physical world rests on the spiritual world. Satan has power to contend prayers if he comprehends them. He contended Daniel's prayers. Had Daniel enveloped his request with tongues of the Spirit the devil wouldn't have reached them. He can't understand requests enabled in the spiritual language.

For if I pray in an unknown tongue, my spirit prayeth, but my understanding is unfruitful. What is it then? I will pray with the spirit, and I will pray with the understanding also: I will sing with the spirit, and I will sing with the understanding also. {I Cor. 14.14,15 KJV}

According to Mark 16.17, the phrases: "…in my name shall they cast out devils…" and "… they shall speak with new tongues" are separated by semi-colons, which implies that they are conjunctive (i.e., they go together). So, don't expect them to cast out devils if their speaking with new tongues is not allowed. Paul the Apostle understood the importance of this, so, in Acts 19.2 he asked a pivotal question. He knew those disciples at Ephesus could not effectively practice the faith except they spoke in tongues. To speak in tongues is not optional. According to Jude 1.20; it builds your faith and your inner man. You don't want to grow without power in the spiritual realm. It will be abnormal to be a believer and be powerless. There can't be life until there is spirit. In John 4.24 and 6.63, "…they are spirit and life…" The trinity does not work in isolation. God the Father speaks, the Son confirms, and the Holy Spirit manifests. The Son confirms because He is the Word. This is why fortifying yourself with the word is a must.

And he was clothed with a vesture dipped in blood: and his name is called The Word of God. (**Revelation 19:13 KJV**)

That confirmeth the word of his servant, and performeth the counsel of his messengers; that saith to Jerusalem, Thou shalt be inhabited; and to the cities of Judah, Ye shall be built, and I will raise up the decayed places thereof: **(Isaiah 44:26 KJV)**

If you are empty of the word, what then does He confirm? You can't also afford to play to the gallery. Because it is the word you speak He puts a seal on. He can't authenticate what is not His. The endorsement is an announcement of the genuineness of the revelation put out. Speak His word, employ His attention. The display of His word invites Him to the scene. Do you want unusual miracles? Put premium on the word. The priority and attention you accord the word matters a great deal.

I will worship toward thy holy temple, and praise thy name for thy lovingkindness and for thy truth: for thou hast magnified thy word above all thy name. {Psalm 138:2 KJV}

8

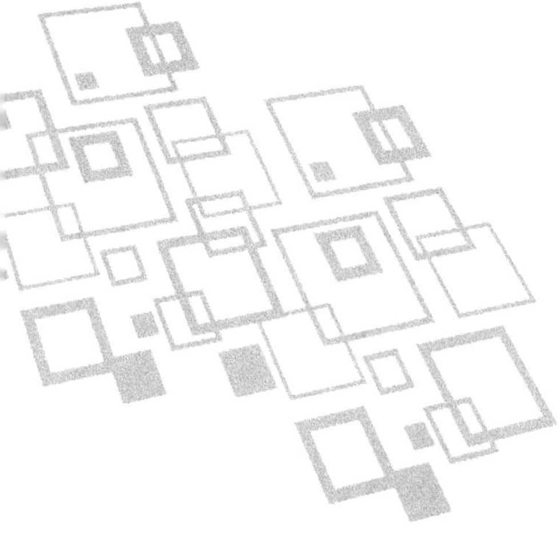

HOLY GHOST BREAKS LIMITS

And it shall come to pass afterward, that I will pour out my spirit upon all flesh; and your sons and your daughters shall prophesy, your old men shall dream dreams, your young men shall see visions: And also upon the servants and upon the handmaids in those days will I pour out my spirit. And I will shew wonders in the heavens and in the earth, blood, and fire, and pillars of smoke. The sun shall be turned into darkness, and the moon into blood, before the great and terrible day of the LORD come. And it shall come to pass, that whosoever shall call on the name of the LORD shall be delivered: for in mount Zion and in Jerusalem shall be deliverance, as the LORD *hath said, and in the remnant whom the* LORD *shall call. {Joel 2:28-32 KJV}*

Nothing best describes the words of the prophet in Joel 2:28-32, like the evacuation of limits. In verse 28, the sons and daughters are expected to prophesy. Have you taken special notice of the words: "sons" and "daughters" it intentionally didn't use the terms "boys" and "girls". The latter connotes gender, while the former speaks of loyalty. The spirit of the prophet only comes on sons and daughters who have been faithful. There is a way you pray for a man, even if he doesn't pray for you formerly, his prophetic anointing comes on you. Unexpectedly, the old men are to consolidate not aspire. Nevertheless, they are to chew out more plans and goals for the future. This effectively means they shall be strong and active. Retrospection comes with amendments of mistakes after long active and engaging years. Normally, that comes in people's later years. So, their chronological ages have been assumed to be immaterial compared to their relevance.

The LORD is my strength and my shield; my heart trusted in him, and I am helped: therefore my heart greatly rejoiceth; and with my song will I praise him. {**Psalm 28:7 KJV**}

The first limit the outpouring has broken is age and gender barriers. In this world, it is not unusual to expect a decline in one's performance with age. But, in this scriptural postulation, the reverse is to be expected. The outpouring of the Holy Spirit makes your age not count against you. You are to age gracefully. Remember in Joshua 14:7-15, it was Caleb who screamed out for this kind of unabated lifestyle. It is a dimension you must move into. God does not expect His anointed to be weakly and sick. You know, Aaron couldn't die until the priestly garment was taken off him. Not even when he went astray.

And strip Aaron of his garments, and put them upon

Eleazar his son: and Aaron shall be gathered unto his people, and shall die there. And Moses did as the LORD commanded: and they went up into mount Hor in the sight of all the congregation. {**Numbers 20:26-27 KJV**}

As long as Aaron wore the garment nothing untoward could touch him. These are realms of glory the anointing brings. How can you carry the presence of God and sickness at the same time? It is an error to enjoy His presence, and then go through rising and falling. You can't enjoy the fullness of the package of the word until the light of it is revealed. Illumination brings liberation, speed, and direction. Furthermore, in Joel 2:28c, "…your young men shall see visions". Nothing enlists a productive youth. The highest targets of Satan in all demography are the youths. It is understandable. If they get it well, the future is secured, and the present is productive. Visions speak of profitable plans and goals for the society. A community develops when the youths are active and productive. This is what exactly prophet Joel foretold about the outpouring. Receiving the Holy Ghost is everything the society needs.

Make you perfect in every good work to do his will, working in you that which is well pleasing in his sight, through Jesus Christ; to whom be glory forever and ever. Amen. {Hebrews 13:21 KJV}

In fact, as a way of emphasis, the Holy Ghost is not limited to church work. How can you house the Holy Ghost and have carryovers? Your business should not dwindle. Your career progression must be smooth and flawless. Unlimited mindset about Him unlocks unlimited expectations from Him. He can do whatever good thing you can think. If you can comprehend it, you can apprehend it. The coming of the Holy Spirit destroys discrimination. Your social class does not matter if you have Him. It elevates you to the class of gods. According to Psalm 82:1, "…ye are gods and sons of the Most High…"

The setting of this authorship of Joel 2:29 is Jewish, where the servants and maids had little or no rights in those days. Therefore, for a prophet to make resounding provisions and promises inclusive of servants and maids is quite outstanding.

And also upon the servants and upon the handmaids in those days will I pour out my spirit. {Joel 2:29 KJV}

In this dispensation of the Holy Ghost, no one has any excuse to fail. Expect wonders in the heavens and the earth equally. The will of God will be seamlessly replicated on earth as it is in heaven. His coming helps you to break limits. Have you been stuck on one spot? The anointing will accelerate you forward. God is after men who are conscious of His kingdom and His house.

But seek ye first the kingdom of God, and his righteousness; and all these things shall be added unto you.{Matthew 6:33KJV}

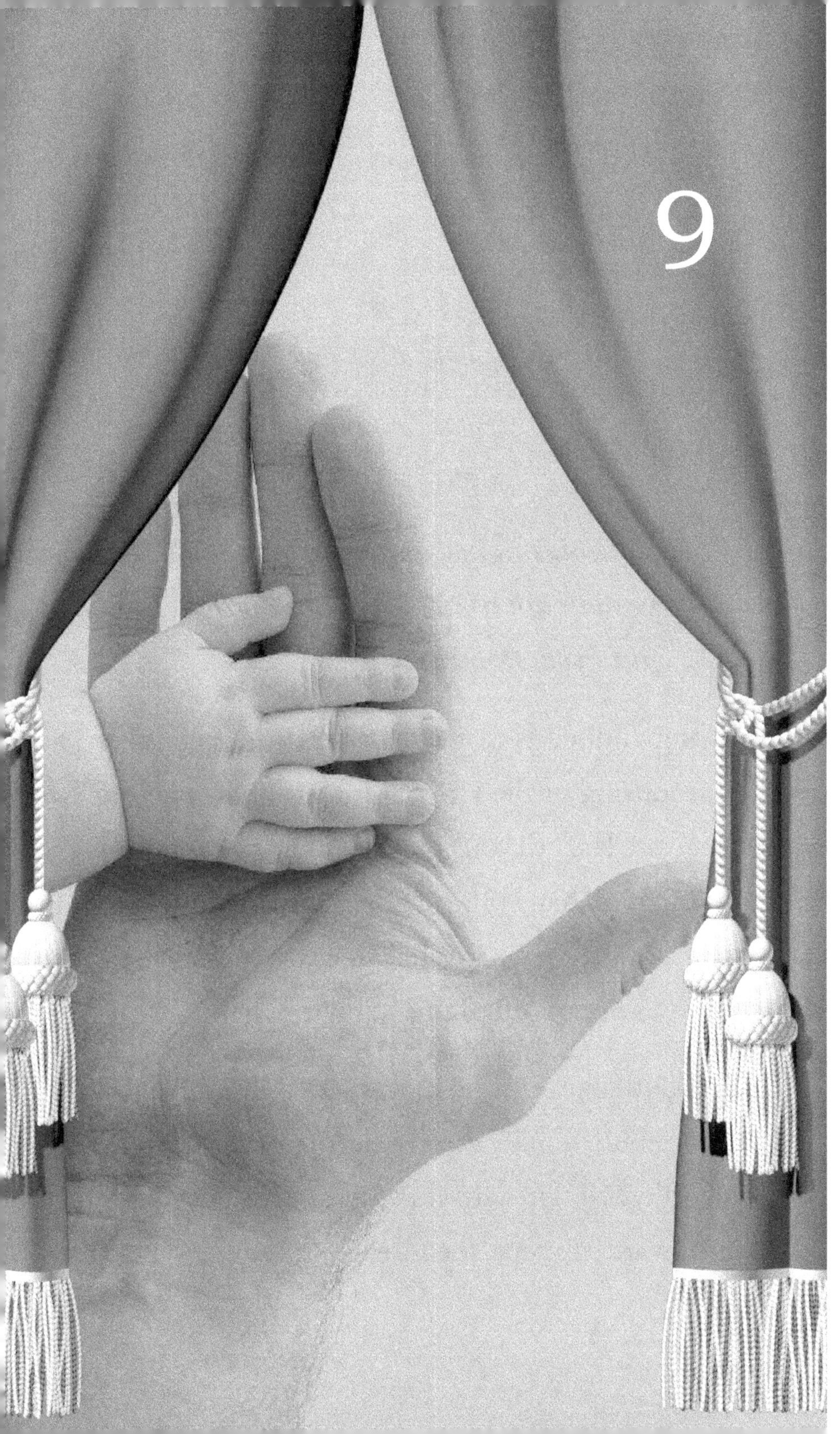
9

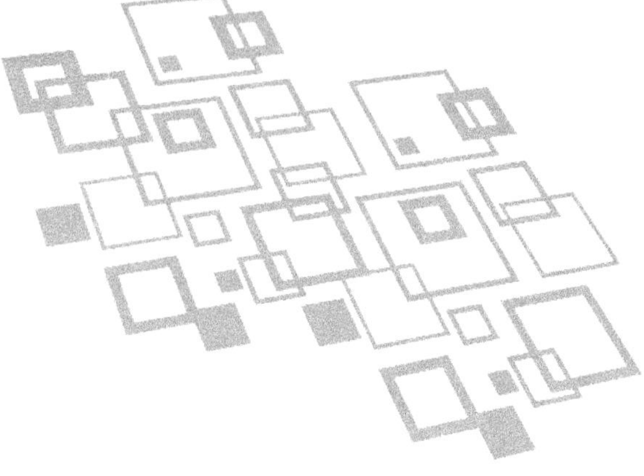

ABIDE IN HIM

If ye abide in me, and my words abide in you, ye shall ask what ye will, and it shall be done unto you. {John 15:7 KJV}

Being endued is easier than remaining endued. The outpouring of the Holy Spirit is not an event, it is a process. The grievous mistake of most believers is the inability to hang on. Any fire that only burns once in a while may have limited usage. Keeping the flame on is as important as initiating the fire.

In Matthew 10:25, Satan was referred to as Beelzebub. Beelzebub literally means the lord of the flies. Typical of flies, if fire drives them away, they return afterward. Except the fire is still there, they then bench. You can't afford to be on fire today and be cold tomorrow. It is disastrous not to be consistent.

Know ye not that they which run in a race run all, but one receiveth the prize? So run, that ye may obtain. And every man that striveth for the mastery is temperate in all things. Now they do it to obtain a corruptible crown; but we an incorruptible. I therefore so run, not as uncertainly; so fight I, not as one that beateth the air: But I keep under my body, and bring it into subjection: lest that by any means, when I have preached to others, I myself should be a castaway. {**I Cor. 9.24-27 KJV**}

The Christian race is a marathon. It is life. The fish can't stay out of the water and survive. The nature of the bird is to fly. It can't do it once and thereafter, celebrate the feat for another period of time. The Lord holds the glory; you only shine when you carry Him. According to Matthew 21:1-5, the donkey enjoyed unprecedented honour as long as it carried the Master. Can you pause a little and imagine that same donkey entering Jerusalem without the Lord

Jesus on its back? Certainly, the donkey will be disappointed.

And when they drew nigh unto Jerusalem, and were come to Bethpage, unto the mount of Olives, then sent Jesus two disciples, Saying unto them, Go into the village over against you, and straightway ye shall find an ass tied, and a colt with her: loose them, and bring them unto me. And if any man say ought unto you, ye shall say, The Lord hath need of them; and straightway he will send them. All this was done, that it might be fulfilled which was spoken by the prophet, saying, Tell ye the daughter of Sion, Behold, thy King cometh unto thee, meek, and sitting upon an ass, and a colt the foal of an ass. And the disciples went, and did as Jesus commanded them, And brought the ass, and the colt, and put on them their clothes, and they set him thereon. And a very great multitude spread their garments in the way; others cut down branches from the trees, and strawed them in the way. And the multitudes that went before, and that followed, cried, saying, Hosanna to the son of David: Blessed is he that cometh in the name of the Lord; Hosanna in the highest. And when he was come into Jerusalem, all the city was moved, saying, who is this? And the multitude said, this is Jesus the prophet of Nazareth of Galilee. (**Matthew 21:1-11 KJV**)

You will reign as long as the Lord of glory is resident in you. Carrying the Master into Jerusalem is a daily affair. The likelihood of meeting a particular uber driver on a given route is almost zero. That you carried the Lord of glory in your last trip doesn't mean you will still meet Him again the next time. Assumption is fatal in this kingdom. Without the Lord Jesus in you, everyone will ignore you. Don't step out of the house except you are sure of His presence. It is foolishness rushing to start the daily activities when the Lord of the day is not present.

Thou wilt shew me the path of life: in thy presence is fulness of joy; at thy right hand there are pleasures for evermore. {**Psalm 16:11 KJV**}

Recall, the great mistake the foster parents of Christ Jesus made when He was about twelve. They left Him behind in the temple.

Now his parents went to Jerusalem every year at the feast of the passover. And when he was twelve years old, they went up to Jerusalem after the custom of the feast. And when they had fulfilled the days, as they returned, the child Jesus tarried behind in Jerusalem; and Joseph and his mother knew not of it. But they, supposing him to have been in the company, went a day's journey; and they sought him among their kinsfolk and acquaintance. And when they found him not, they turned back again to Jerusalem, seeking him. {Luke 2:41-45 KJV}

How many believers see the Holy Spirit as church display euphoria nowadays? In some extreme cases, the bold–faced rascality has even extended to the church. In Luke 2:41-45, there are lessons to learn. Firstly, no matter how far you have gone, retrace your steps if you have left the Master behind. Joseph and Mary returned back to the temple as soon as they could not find Christ Jesus (Luke 2:45). A day's journey could have amounted to several kilometers. The distance covered already without His presence is immaterial.

Secondly, the mistake of embarking on a journey without Jesus could have been avoided. Joseph and Mary survived that mistake, several others couldn't. How do you step out of a house without due approval from Him? If He must be Lord, He must be Lord of everything. Stop using your brain to calculate everything. You must be mindful of what He is saying at every given point in time. What He said yesterday, might not be what He is saying now. Being anointed is being current in the Spirit.

Ye call me Master and Lord: and ye say well; for so I am. If I then, your Lord and Master, have washed your feet; ye also ought to wash one another's feet. **{John 13:13-14 KJV}**

1.   Notice

If you must abide in Him; you must learn to notice. Noticing is linked to observation. Sometimes, God may not outrightly tell you everything audibly. He expects you to observe the changes He has occasioned around you. In II Kings 4:9, the Shunem woman displayed this trait. She acted in line with the will of God, because she could perceive.

And it fell on a day, that Elisha passed to Shunem, where was a great woman; and she constrained him to eat bread. And so it was, that as oft as he passed by, he turned in thither to eat bread. And she said unto her husband, Behold now, I perceive that this is an holy man of God, which passeth by us continually. {II Kings 4:8-9 KJV}

Actually, God allowed Elisha to pass that route for her to be blessed. You must be spiritual enough to see fertile land. When last did you observe a fertile land to sow into?

(2)   Question

One of the signs of knowledgeable people is the propensity to know. Learn to ask questions. Seeking clarification shows you put premium on excellence. Don't run into avoidable errors. Had Christ Jesus not asked where they could buy bread, perhaps, the lad would not have been discovered.

In Matthew 16:13-20, He, again, sought their opinion of what men took Him for. Christ Jesus could know these answers even before asking. However, He gave opportunity to the disciples to express themselves. Don't assume He permitted you to take a similar step before. Verify again before acting.

And Jesus went out, and his disciples, into the towns of Caesarea Philippi: and by the way he asked his disciples, saying unto them, Whom do men say that I am? {**Mark 8:27 KJV**}

(3). Respond

Response requires awareness, reflection, curiosity, humility, and the commitment to relate to each other. Sometimes, response may require you to admit wrong. You must never be ashamed to be wrong. Be open-minded enough to know that you're a mortal man who can still make mistakes. So, self-awareness of your strengths and weaknesses is important. Knowledge of yourself empowers your prayer life. Presumption will only destroy greatness. Therefore, learn to stay aside and reflect on the events around. The voice of the Lord will always speak if only you remain teachable.

Likewise, ye younger, submit yourselves unto the elder. Yea, all of you be subject one to another, and be clothed with humility: for God resisteth the proud, and giveth grace to the humble. {I Peter 5:5 KJV}